GIRl

Josephine Cox was born in Blackburn, and was one of ten children. She met and married her husband Ken when she was sixteen, and had two sons. When the boys started school, she decided to go to college and got a place at Cambridge University. She didn't accept it because she would have had to live away from home. Instead she went into teaching – and started to write her first book. She won the 'Superwoman of Great Britain' Award in 1987, for which her family had entered her secretly, at the same time as her novel was accepted for publication.

Her strong, gritty stories are based on real life. Josephine says, 'I could never imagine a single day without writing. It's been that way since as far back as I can remember.'

Visit www.josephinecox.co.uk to read her exclusive serial, catch up with her online diary and to find out more information about Josephine.

You can also visit www.AuthorTracker.co.uk for exclusive updates on Josephine Cox.

Argyll and Bute Libraries

34115 00410507 4

Also by Josephine Cox

JOSEPHINE COX

Girl on the Platform

HARPER

HarperCollins*Publishers*
77–85 Fulham Palace Road,
Hammersmith, London W6 8JB

www.harpercollins.co.uk

Published by HarperCollins*Publishers* 2008
1

Copyright © Josephine Cox 2008

Josephine Cox asserts the moral right to
be identified as the author of this work

A catalogue record for this book
is available from the British Library

ISBN: 978 0 00 727008 8

This novel is entirely a work of fiction.
The names, characters and incidents portrayed in it are
the work of the author's imagination. Any resemblance to
actual persons, living or dead, events or localities is
entirely coincidental.

Set in Stone Serif by Palimpsest Book Production Limited,
Grangemouth, Stirlingshire

Printed and bound in Great Britain by
Clays Ltd, St Ives plc

All rights reserved. No part of this publication may be
reproduced, stored in a retrieval system, or transmitted,
in any form or by any means, electronic, mechanical,
photocopying, recording or otherwise, without the prior
permission of the publishers.

Mixed Sources
Product group from well-managed
forests and other controlled sources
www.fsc.org Cert no. SW-COC-1806
© 1996 Forest Stewardship Council
FSC

FSC is a non-profit international organisation established
to promote the responsible management of the world's forests.
Products carrying the FSC label are independently certified
to assure consumers that they come from forests that are managed
to meet the social, economic and ecological needs
of present and future generations.

Find out more about HarperCollins and the environment at
www.harpercollins.co.uk/green

This book is for my Ken, as always

ARGYLL & BUTE LIBRARIES	
0410507	
HJ	12/02/2008
	£1.99
OBAN	

PART ONE

Friday
August 2007
Woburn Sands

Boys' Night Out

Chapter One

'A night in London?' Mark had never been to the city. 'That sounds good to me.'

'Great!' Pete slapped him on the shoulder. 'I promise you, we'll have a cracking time, but you'd better be ready and waiting, or I'll go on my own.'

'You *won't*!'

'Just watch me!'

'All right, keep your shirt on. I'll be ready.'

At first, Mark wasn't sure if he wanted to go to London and see a show. His idea of a good night out was down the pub, enjoying a pint of beer and a game of pool. If he pulled that was a bonus, but Pete had convinced him and now he was really looking forward to it.

Pete explained the plan. 'Remember, you'll need to be here by six-thirty or we'll miss the train.'

Pete was fed up with the same old routine – go to work, come home, have your tea. Then down the pub. And now that Cathy had finished with him *again*, he was feeling miserable. So when his dad won two tickets to the hit show *Joseph*, he gave them to Pete. 'Take Mark with you,' he said, 'it'll make a change for you both.'

Pete thought it was a great idea. This was the last day of his holiday, and he really needed to do something different before he went back to work on Monday.

As agreed, Mark drove up in his old Ford at exactly six-thirty. Pete told him to park it on the street: 'So Dad can get in and out of the drive.'

Mark looked Pete up and down. 'Get you!' He noted Pete's new jeans and black leather jacket. 'Hope you didn't go to all that trouble for me!'

'Not likely?' Surprisingly though, Mark had made an effort. His fair hair was newly cropped, and he was wearing a black jacket and a pair of really skinny jeans that made his size ten feet stick out like barges.

'Come on then!' Mark was already walking out the door. 'Let's see if London night-life is all it's cracked up to be.'

'Don't go wandering down dark alleys!' Pete's dad called after them. 'You never know who's about.'

'Aw, Dad! I'm not a kid anymore,' Pete told

him. 'In case you've forgotten, I was twenty-five last birthday. I can look after myself.'

Mark squared his shoulders. 'If anybody tries to pick *my* wallet, they'll be sorry!' Punching the air with a clenched fist he quipped, 'One look at me and they'll run a mile.'

Pete told him not to be so cocky. 'You'll only be asking for trouble. Just remember, we're not out to pick a fight. We're out to enjoy ourselves and to check out the sights and pleasures.'

'What *"sights and pleasures"*?'

Pete had to think hard about that. 'Well, *I* don't know, do I? All I'm saying is lots of people think London is the place to be, so now's our chance to find out.'

'What time is the last train back?' Mark asked.

'Why do you want to know that?' Pete groaned.

'I don't want to be stranded in London, that's all.'

'We won't be,' Pete promised. 'So stop asking what time we'll get back, when we haven't even *got* there yet.'

At the top of Russell Street, they came onto the High Street, and then it was a five minute walk down to the train station.

Pete checked his watch. 'We change at Milton Keynes and get the seven-thirty to Euston. Then we can get a taxi to the theatre. After the show, we'll suss out the area . . . find a night club. Get a taste of London. Then it's back in a taxi to the station, and make our way home.'

Mark had another idea. 'Let's make a night of it. We could always find a hotel.'

Pete thought about that for a minute. 'How much money have you got?'

Mark peered into his wallet. 'Well, I paid Mum her board, and I owed Dad a tenner from last week; and I've got the train and taxi fare.' Closing his wallet, he grumbled, 'You're right. Maybe we can't afford a hotel, but I'm sure we could find a cheap bed and breakfast.'

Pete was not sure. 'How much have you got altogether?'

Mark didn't hear. He was too busy counting his coins.

'*MARK*!' Pete asked again. 'Come on, mate. Exactly how much have you got to spend?'

'Well, if you take out a fiver for a drink in the interval . . . I'll have about twenty quid.'

'*How* much?' Pete could hardly believe his ears.

'You heard.'

'*Twenty quid*!' Pete groaned. 'So, after the train and the taxi, and a drink during the interval, you're left with just twenty quid?' He gave Mark a curious glance. 'Did you get your wages today?'

'Of course!'

Pete's heart sank. 'Don't tell me . . . you've been backing the horses again, haven't you?'

'So what if I have?' Mark had a weakness for gambling, which he was trying to control. 'It's *my* money isn't it?'

'I thought you said you would never back another horse. Especially after last week, when you lost loads on that old nag. What was it called, oh yes . . . *Highway to Heaven*!'

'I suppose you think I'm on the highway to hell, don't you?'

Pete shook his head, 'Course not. It's just that you'll never have any money if you keep gambling.'

'I know that.' Mark also knew he had a real problem. 'I can't help it. Some people are addicted to drink and cigarettes or women. *I'm* addicted to betting on the horses. I *will* stop though. I *have* to.' He knew he had to give it up, or he would find himself in real trouble.

Pete understood. 'All right, I know you've been trying, and I guess it won't be easy. You're bound to slip up now and then. Look . . . if I can help in any way, you've only to ask. I'll keep your wages for you if you like. Or maybe when you get paid, we can go out . . . somewhere where you can't back the horses.

'Every time you feel the urge to throw your money away at the bookies, call me, or come round, and we'll go somewhere to take your mind off it. Wherever I am, I'll be there for you.'

His voice hardened. 'Just remember though . . . I will *not* help you, if you don't help yourself. And I won't lend you *my* hard-earned money to waste. Okay?'

'Okay.'

'Right then. So get a move on, because the gates are closed and the train's coming in!'

The two of them set off at a run, and managed to scramble on board the train just as it was about to leave.

Mark threw himself into the seat. 'Another minute and we would never have made it!'

Pete wasn't listening. Instead, his attention was taken by a girl on the opposite platform, 'I wouldn't mind getting to know *her*.' Seated on a bench was a young woman in her early twenties. 'She looks a bit sad though, don't you think?'

Mark laughed. 'She's probably broke . . . like me. Maybe she's addicted to backing horses as well.'

As the train moved away, Mark tapped on the window, trying to catch her attention. 'Hey! I'll cheer you up if you want!' he called out. 'You and me could go to the races . . . what do you say to that?'

When the man opposite glared at him, Mark slunk in his seat. 'Miserable old git!' he grumbled. 'I bet he's never enjoyed himself in his life!'

Leaning forward, Pete warned him to keep his voice down. 'What makes you think he's never enjoyed himself?'

'You only have to *look* at the poor old sod!'

The man was small and shrunk, with a balding head and a hangdog face. He scowled at Mark, then he opened his satchel and, taking out a small laptop computer, he began tapping away.

'Oh look, here we go!' Mark rolled his eyes to heaven. 'Boring old geezers, head-bent to their laptops . . . tap-tap-tapping away. Then mobile phones will start ringing. Everybody knows everybody else's business . . . what they had for breakfast, or if they've had an argument with their other half. After that, they'll be bragging about how they've just cut a deal worth millions, when all the time they're just ordinary grafters, like you and me!

'Eric Peters from the warehouse says he learned more about life and sex from listening to people chatting on their mobiles than he ever learned from experience.'

Pete wasn't listening. He had been stretching his neck to catch sight of the girl on the bench. 'What did you say?'

'What's up with you?' Mark gave him a kick. 'You're not even listening, are you?'

Pete didn't answer. He was still looking at the girl, and though every minute took him further away, he had managed to get a good look at her. Even though her long, dark hair hid part of her face, he had still seen enough to suspect that she was unhappy.

He had known prettier girls, and this one was not beautiful by any means. But she wasn't plain, and she had a kind of endearing quality, which had drawn him to her. From what he could see, she had a small, shapely figure, a lovely full mouth, and pretty eyes, which looked up only once, to check the monitor for train arrivals. The rest of the time she had been looking down at the ground, head bent and deep in thought.

She had not seen him, and he was glad about that, because she might have been upset to see him staring at her. In that split second when she *did* look up, his heart turned somer-saults. No other girl had ever affected him like that.

'PETE!' Mark shook him by the shoulder. 'Get a grip! You've done nothing but stare at that girl. What's so special about her anyway?'

Pete shrugged. 'Nothing in particular, I suppose.' He didn't want to tell Mark how he felt. 'She just caught my eye, that's all.'

'Forget *her!* There'll be so many girls in London, we won't know which way to turn. Anyway . . . that girl back there, well, she looked a bit too miserable for my liking. I prefer women with a bit more life to them. A bit of fun, that's what we want.'

He gave Pete another kick. 'Am I right, or am I right?'

Pete nodded. 'You're right!'

The train had swung away and he could not see the girl any more. 'I see what you mean . . . I don't suppose I should be wasting time over one lonely girl. This is *our* night out.' He tried to push her out of his mind. 'What's *one* girl compared to what London might have to offer?'

Mark laughed out loud. '*Now* you're talking!'

Excited and full of plans for the evening, Mark chatted on.

Pete nodded, saying yes and no where needed, but try as he might, he could not ignore the image in his mind. Truth was, the girl on the platform had really got to him.

Chapter Two

For the next hour Pete and Mark were busy making plans for the evening. 'I reckon we should go to Soho,' Mark suggested. 'Eric Peters says it's where all the best night clubs are.'

'How does he know?'

'He got to know London pretty well when he was on a course there, plus his mates took him to London for his stag-night last year. They stayed at some place near Soho, and they partied all night! Apparently, the clubs were well lively, and all the girls were out for a good time.'

Pete liked the idea of that. 'All right then. Like I said, after the theatre, we'll head for the clubs. Okay?' After seeing the girl on the platform he needed to clear his mind.

'Great!' Then Mark had another idea. 'Why don't we give the theatre a miss, and go straight to the clubs?'

'No. We'll go and see the show like we planned. There'll be time enough for the clubs,' Pete told him.

'Yes, but we've got to find somewhere to stay the night. By the time we've done that and then gone to the show, there won't be much time left for clubbing, will there?' Mark was disappointed. 'Why do you want to see *Joseph* anyway?'

Pete explained, 'Because my dad gave us the tickets so we could see the show. Anyway, I thought *you* wanted to see it? If I remember rightly, it was *you* who watched the talent competition on TV from start to finish. *You* were the one who voted for that Lee bloke to win, and now you've got the chance to see him on stage. So what's the problem?'

'I've never been to a musical before.'

'Yes, and now you can . . . thanks to my dad.'

'But what if I don't like it? What if I want to come out halfway through?'

'You won't.'

'Okay, so what if I make it to the end, and it's really late when we get to the clubs? All the best looking girls will be taken.'

'That won't happen.'

'How can you be so sure?'

'*Think* about it,' Pete urged. 'When we get off the train, we'll get the taxi driver to drive us to a B&B. Then after we've checked in, we'll grab a bite to eat and make our way to the

14

theatre. We'll be out of the theatre well before midnight, so by the time we get to the clubs, they'll be hotting up.'

Mark grinned. 'D'you reckon?'

'Too right!' Pete assured him. 'You'll have the girls swooning all over you.'

Mark laughed out loud. 'Sounds good to me!'

For a time they sat quietly. Mark closed his eyes and thought about the wonderful night he was in for, and all the good looking girls he was going to meet.

Pete gazed out of the window. Like Mark, he was really looking forward to checking out London night-life. But he felt strangely uneasy. His thoughts were still back there, with the girl on the platform. She had stirred memories in him, painful memories that he would much rather have forgotten. Memories of another girl, younger, cruel and cold; his first real love.

Mark saw Pete lost in thought, and he was intrigued. 'Hey, you!'

Pete looked up. 'What?'

'You look awful. Anybody would think you were going to the gallows, instead of heading for the best time of your life. What's wrong with you?'

'Just thinking, that's all,' he gestured out of the window. 'Why don't you carry on looking at the scenery,' he suggested, '. . . and leave me alone?'

'Suit yourself!'

Mark returned his attention to the landscape, but it was only a moment before Pete started to apologise. 'Sorry, mate. It's just that, well, the girl back there on the platform . . .' He looked away.

'What about her?' Mark sensed Pete was about to confide in him. 'I saw how taken you were with her . . . fancy her don't you?' He grinned, not expecting for a moment what Pete was about to confide in him.

'I know it sounds mad but . . . she sort of reminds me of myself,' Pete began quietly. 'That's what drew me to her.' He smiled. 'There's something about her . . .'

Intrigued, Mark leaned forward in his seat. 'What did you mean just then?'

'When?'

'Just now . . . when you said she reminded you of yourself?'

'Nothing!' Pete was wishing he had kept his thoughts to himself. 'Just forget it!'

'No!' Mark urged him on. 'C'mon . . . what did you mean?'

Pete took a long, noisy breath and paused for a second or two. Then he began to voice his thoughts. 'She looked wounded . . . like she'd been hurt by somebody . . .'

Mark joked, 'What . . . like she's had a row with her parents . . . or something? Sorry, mate, it's tough but we all have to deal with life's little crises.'

Pete gave him a shrivelling glance. 'You've no idea, have you?' There was a touch of envy in his voice.

Mark had never seen Pete like this. 'She's really got to you, hasn't she? What's on your mind – what's all this about? Is there something you're not telling me?'

Pete looked him in the eye. 'I reckon she's been hurt like I was seven years ago,' he confided. 'It seems like yesterday, I remember it so clearly. It took me a long time to get over it.'

'Get over *what* for pity's sake?'

Pete told him. 'I was working at Jason's car-parts warehouse. There was me and three other blokes in the warehouse, and two girls working the phones.'

He gave a slow, wry little smile. 'Then Claire was taken on to man the office. She was bright, funny and genuine. To cut a long story short,

I invited everyone to my eighteenth birthday party, including her. We got on really well and we started going out. She was the first girl I fell in love with.'

'Wow.' Mark was impressed. You don't waste time. So, what happened?'

Pete continued, 'Claire was my first real sweetheart, and to be honest, I worshipped the ground she walked on . . . bought her things, and did everything she wanted. Anyway, it was a month or so later, when I took her to Barney's Club in town. She got a bit drunk and when it was time to take her home she laughed in my face and then I couldn't find her . . . she just disappeared.'

Remembering how it had been was still painful after all this time. 'I searched everywhere for her . . . asked everybody if they'd seen her but nobody had. Then one of the girls told me she'd seen Claire about an hour before, making her way to the cloakrooms.' He shrugged his shoulders, 'I heard a noise at the back of the cloakrooms and there she was, with Jack from the warehouse. I thought he was a mate, but it turned out that was the second biggest mistake I'd made. The two of them had been together even before she started at the warehouse, and between the two of them they had milked me for every penny I'd got. They were laughing at me behind my back.' He looked out the window. 'It was all a big joke to them.'

Mark was shocked. 'So what did you do?'

Pete smiled. 'The only thing I *could* do! I just walked away, from her, from my work.' He shrugged his shoulders, but Mark could see the shame on his face. 'A clean sheet, and a lesson learned.'

'Right!' Mark had never been let down like that, but he realised how it might damage somebody, especially at eighteen. 'So, you think that girl on the platform had something like that happen to her?'

Pete shrugged again. 'Dunno, but I recognise that look,' he admitted. 'Kind of faraway, not really caring.' He grinned suddenly. 'I might be totally wrong, and she's just wondering what to have for tea. But, I do know this much . . .'

'What?'

'I'm going to see her again.'

Mark warned him. 'Beware strange girls. If you're not careful, they'll eat you for breakfast!'

Pete laughed aloud. 'Shut up, lunatic!'

'Hey!' Mark jolted him out of his moodiness. 'So, you really think we'll score tonight then?' Rubbing his hands together, he gave Pete a cheeky smile.

'I've already said, haven't I?' He had already forgotten about the girl who cheated on him with a mate – though the image of the girl on the platform lingered. 'Hey! Tonight might be the night when you meet your future wife. Have you thought of that?'

Mark was horrified. 'I'm not looking for a future wife. I haven't got time to settle down, not when I can pick and choose.'

Pete wagged a finger. 'One of these days, some girl will come along, and sweep you off your feet.'

'No way!' Mark had no wish to be tied to one woman. 'I'm a free spirit . . . born to play the field.'

When Pete lapsed into silence again, Mark gave him a curious glance. 'What's up?'

'What do you mean?'

'Well, you seem miles away . . . *again*!'

'Just thinking.'

'About what?'

'Not about . . . what happened,' Pete assured him. 'That's all in the past.'

'You're not worried about me and the gambling are you, because if you are . . .'

'I'm not,' Pete assured him. 'You're doing all right.'

Mark felt proud. 'Really?'

'Yes, really. Okay, you've had a few slip-ups, but that's bound to happen, before you get the better of it.'

'You reckon I'll beat it then?' Mark valued Pete's support.

'I do, yes.'

'So, you don't think I'm a loser?'

'No! When have I ever said that?'

'Well, you haven't,' Mark admitted. 'You've always helped me. Even when I was at my lowest, owing money everywhere and lying to you so you'd help me out, you never asked questions. You never judged me, and you never lectured me.'

He looked at Pete, and he was grateful he had this long-time friend. 'You know what?'

'What?'

'I think I'd have sunk without trace, if you hadn't bailed me out.'

'You'd do the same for me, wouldn't you?'

Mark smiled knowingly. 'I would never have to,' he answered. 'You wouldn't get yourself into such a mess in the first place.'

'Oh, I've had my moments, don't think I haven't.'

'What ... *gambling*, you mean?' Mark was astonished.

'No, not exactly gambling, but near enough I suppose.'

'So, if it wasn't gambling, what was it then?'

'Going on Ebay. I was at the computer every minute, buying this and that, bidding for stuff I didn't even need.'

'You never told me.'

'It was soon after you moved into the street. We didn't know each other too well back then.'

'So, what did you do?'

'I sold my computer.'

'So, how come you've got one *now?*'

'My plan was to be without a computer for a while, and it worked. During those few months when I was without one, the addiction went away.'

'That's what I mean. You're different from me, you make a plan and stick to it.'

'So will you ... once you've made up your mind.'

Changing the subject, Mark began to chat excitedly. 'I feel like this could be my lucky night,' he bragged. 'They say if you feel lucky, you'll *be* lucky.' He gave a stifled cry. 'Yes! Mark's in town! Come on you babes!'

He would have gone on talking, but Pete threw him a newspaper that he'd found lying on the opposite seat. 'Here. Calm down and read the paper.'

While Mark buried his head in the newspaper, Pete leaned back in his seat and gave himself up to the rhythm of the train as it rumbled along, making a tune as it clattered over the rails – 'Who's the girl – Who's the girl' – it sang as it went; try as he might, he could not get her out of his mind.

'Come on, Pete,' he muttered to himself, 'stop dreaming! You'll probably never see her again.'

Mark raised his face from the newspaper. 'Are you talking to *me?*'

Pete shook his head. 'No.'

Mark returned to the racing pages.

After a time, Pete was relieved to see that Mark had turned the page, and was now absorbed in an article on coloured hair-gel.

Chapter Three

In no time at all, they had arrived at Euston and were clambering off the train with a sea of rushing passengers. 'Come on!' Pushing through the crowds, they hurried along. 'Quick, Mark!' Pete yanked him forward, 'the taxi-rank is over there.' He pointed to the far end of the shopping area.

With the crowd surging up behind them, they shuffled down the steps, then along the corridor, and now they were at the top of the steps to the underground. 'Look! There are plenty of taxis.' Mark peered over the handrail at the ever-moving row of taxis below.

'Maybe, but there are still more people than taxis,' Pete said, giving him a little shove. 'Keep moving.'

In a surprisingly short time they were climbing into a black cab. 'Do you know any cheap B&Bs?' Pete asked, the taxi driver.

'Somewhere close to Soho.' Mark chipped in, 'in case we get too drunk to find our way back . . .'

'Ssh!' Pete gave him a dig in the ribs. 'He's right though. It would be good to get somewhere within walking distance of the centre. It *would* save us money on a taxi back.'

'I just might be able to help you out there.' The driver started the engine and inched forward, one ear pressed to his mobile phone. 'That's right ... two young men, just the one night. Yes, they look okay.'

He glanced in his mirror to observe his two passengers. He thought Pete seemed like a regular, responsible guy, with his cropped brown hair and dark, sincere eyes. He seemed to have an easy, quiet way with him too. His gaze lingered on Mark, who seemed a bit edgy. 'You're not out to cause trouble, are you?'

'Absolutely not!' Mark was offended. 'We're just out for a night in London.'

The driver returned to his conversation. 'No, they seem all right. The blond-haired one is a bit lippy.'

Mark leaned forward. 'What's that supposed to mean?'

'It means what it says ... you've got a bit too much lip on you.'

'You're right,' Pete intervened. 'I'm always telling him ... he doesn't know when to shut it.'

'Oh, that's right!' Folding his arms, Mark

slunk back into his seat. 'Gang up on me, why don't you?'

The driver explained, 'No offence meant, mate. The only place you'll get bed and breakfast near Soho is at my sister's guest house. I'm just making sure I don't take a heap of trouble to her door.' He laughed out loud. 'Mind you she's no pushover. Right from when we were kids, she'd always get the upper hand.

'There are five of us . . . two girls and three boys. Leila might be the youngest, but she's the fieriest . . . it's the *Italian* blood you know.'

For a moment, he concentrated his attention on the traffic lights ahead. Once they had rounded the corner, he continued, 'As I was saying, two of my brothers got in a fight with some kids from the East End. They were getting the worst of it, when the word got back to Leila. She kicked off her shoes and ran barefoot all the way there.'

'So, what happened?' Mark asked.

'She just launched herself at them . . . biting and scratching like a wildcat. We heard later, she'd bitten off a part of one of their ears.'

'Bloody hell! She sounds like a mad woman!' Wide-eyed and frantic, Mark looked at Pete. 'I think we should look for somewhere else to stay the night!'

Pete laughed. 'Stop worrying. If you behave yourself, you might get away in the morning, with both ears intact.'

'Look at it this way,' the driver grinned at him in the mirror, 'you couldn't be in safer hands. If anybody gives you trouble while she's around, they'll rue the day.'

When he dropped them off outside a Victorian house, Mark lingered outside. 'Fighting off two boys . . . she's either off her rocker or she's built like an outhouse!'

'She doesn't worry me!' Pete sounded confident, but he didn't feel it.

'Liar!' Mark pushed him up the steps. 'If you're so brave, you can go first!'

'All right, I will!' Pete told him boldly. 'Why should we be frightened of her anyway? We're here to enjoy ourselves, not to cause trouble. All I want is to check in, freshen up a bit, and head off to the theatre.'

While Mark hung back, Pete rang the doorbell.

'What do you want?' The young woman who opened the door looked to be in her early twenties. She was strikingly beautiful, with wild dark hair and a smile that momentarily lit up the street. She was obviously expecting someone else, because when she saw Pete and Mark, her smile slid away and her attitude was less welcoming. 'I have no time to waste,' she grumbled, 'so please, have the good manners to answer my question. Why are you here?'

Lost for words, Pete stared at her. 'Er . . .' he took a deep breath, 'we're here to check in for the night.'

The young woman stepped out, her curious gaze sweeping over Pete, and then behind him, to where Mark was looking at her with his mouth wide open. 'The taxi driver . . . spoke with . . . the owner – your mother,' he stammered, thrown by her fierce good looks and wishing he'd taken more trouble with his appearance. She was fantastic! He felt his stomach rise to his chin, and he was trembling inside. 'We were told you had a couple of rooms available.'

'Really?' Giving Mark the whisper of a smile, and a look that sent him weak at the knees, she looked from him to Pete. Then swinging away towards the door, she instructed in her strong Italian accent, 'You may come along!'

Like meek little lambs, and with Mark not knowing what had hit him, they followed her inside.

She led them to the small desk in the lobby, where she took out a ledger from underneath the counter. Flinging it open, she pushed it towards Pete. 'Sign here.' She pointed to Mark who was still hanging back behind Pete, 'You too.'

Handing them each a pen, she explained, 'Your rooms are numbers ten and twelve, on the first floor. Breakfast is between eight and ten-thirty. After that, there is no food to be served. And there are rules.'

'What kind of rules?' Mark felt uneasy.

'*Strict* rules!' She stared him out. 'There will be no shouting or fighting; no peeing in the handbasin, and no being sick on the carpets. You will not steal the towels when you leave, or pinch the loo-rolls, and you are absolutely not allowed to bring women back here.'

'It's worse than the Foreign Legion!' Mark muttered.

Giving him a disapproving glance, she demanded, 'Do you mean to defy my rules?'

'Absolutely not!' While oddly smitten with this magnificent woman, Mark maintained his refuge behind Pete. 'I would *never* defy your rules!'

Again she turned to smile at him, and when he smiled back, her cheeks coloured.

Having both signed the register, Pete told her, 'My friend might seem a bit odd but he's normally well behaved. Later though, we'll be going out clubbing, so what time does your mother lock the front door?'

'My *mother*?' She lowered her gaze. 'I have no mother.' Her voice trembled, as though she was about to cry; but then in the next minute, she was laying down the law.

'These are *my* premises. *I* make the rules, and *I* am telling you both, the front door will be locked at one minute past midnight. If you shout, or bang on the door and make a nuisance of yourself, I will call the police and have you taken away!'

Mark was stunned. '*Midnight!*' he groaned. 'It's too early! Clubs stay open till the early hours . . . we'll have to leave at half-past eleven to get back here on time!' He appealed to Pete for help. 'Tell her, Pete. It's too early!'

When Pete made no comment, she turned to him. 'Well? What have *you* to say?'

'He's right,' Pete argued. 'It *is* too early, and we were really looking forward to checking out London night-life.'

'So, you're telling me you don't want to stay here?'

'No! I mean . . . well, yes. Can't you please change the rules, just this once?'

Mark was ready to leave. 'We'd best look for

somewhere else,' he said. 'She's not gonna change her mind.'

'You are free to go if that's what you want!' she told them both. 'I do not change my rules for anyone. This door will be locked at midnight. I must warn you though, my guest house is the only one close to Soho; the main hotels are much further away. They are also very expensive, and you will not get service with a smile, like here. Also, you must pay the taxi to get you to the clubs and back again . . . that is, if you can even *find* a taxi in the early hours. It's very difficult you know.'

She slammed the ledger shut. 'I see your mind is made up. So, goodbye. I'm sorry I could not help you.'

Sweeping past them, she opened the front door and gestured for them to leave. 'Please go now.'

'Hey, hang on a minute!' Pete was panicking. 'Just give us a minute to talk.'

'Why?'

'Because I need to persuade my friend.'

'Talk then!' Closing the door, she remained on guard. 'Please, make it quick. I have work piling up.'

Taking Mark aside, Pete said, 'Look mate, we've only got so much money. So, this is the choice.

We either spend the bulk of our money on taxis, and hotel rooms that cost the earth. Then when we've had our little night out, we'll be lucky to find a taxi that will take us back again. That's if we've enough money left to pay for it!'

Mark was really fed-up now. 'So, what do you suggest?'

'I think we should stay here,' Pete decided. 'It means we'll have to be back by midnight, and I'm not happy about that either, but at least we'll have a bit more money to enjoy what time we've got.'

'I don't like the idea of getting back here by midnight!' Mark moaned.

'Neither do I, but what choice do we have?'

Mark was still hopeful that she might change her mind. 'Ask her if she'll just give us an extra hour. Tell her we really will go somewhere else if she doesn't help us out.'

'*NO!*' The landlady had overheard them. 'I do *not* change the rules for you or anyone. I already told you ... the door is locked and bolted on the stroke of midnight. Go or stay, you decide now.'

With very little choice in the matter, the boys decided to stay.

Before she would hand over the keys, she had another rule. 'Payment in advance, please.'

'What!' Mark was ready for an argument.

'You pay me now, or you leave.'

'That's ridiculous!'

'You pay me *now!*' Her dark eyes flashed with anger. 'If I don't have my money now, how do I know you will still be here tomorrow morning?'

'Because we give you our word.'

'Your word is no good to me! Your word will not pay my bills.' When she shook her head, her wild dark curls swung across her face, and once again Mark couldn't help but notice how pretty she was. 'I don't even know who you are!' she snapped. She began brandishing the pen. 'How do I know you won't run off?'

'Because we always pay our way!' Pete tried to calm the situation.

She brandished the keys in his face. 'Do you want the keys?'

'Of course!'

'Then you pay me *now!*'

Mark stepped forward. 'We're not thieves.'

She gave a wry little smile. 'And I am not a charity!'

'Don't you trust anyone?'

'Never.'

She watched them as they counted out the money, then she swooped it away and handed them the keys. 'The lift is out of action,' she said happily, 'you will please find the stairs at the bottom of the hall.'

Climbing the steep, narrow stairs was like climbing Everest. 'She's a bit of a nut case,' Pete remarked.

'Maybe she is.' Mark was remembering her dark, moody eyes.

Pete laughed aloud. 'It sounds like you fancy her. You don't . . . do you?'

Mark sighed. 'You have to agree, she's a good-looking woman . . . all that Italian passion.'

Pete grinned. 'I could see you were eyeing her up and down, and so could she.' He gave a sideways grin. 'I reckon she might fancy you an' all.'

Mark blushed to the roots of his hair, 'Give over.'

'I've never seen you so smitten,' Pete said.

'Well, do you blame me? She's got the perfect figure; and long, thick hair you want to run your hands through; oh, and she's got a mouth to die for. I tell you, Pete . . . I wouldn't mind kissing her.'

'More fool you!' Pete reminded him of the taxi-driver's story. 'Don't forget how she took a bite out of that kid's ear.'

Mark gave a sly little chuckle. 'You needn't

worry,' he boasted, 'she would never bite *my* ear off. She'd be far too busy, checking out my body.'

Both Pete and Mark were unaware that Leila was standing at the foot of the stairs, listening to every word.

She went quietly away. 'So, you're the one, are you? My brother was right . . . you *do* seem like a bit of a handful.'

She quickened her step, her eyes alight with mischief. 'I think I should teach you a lesson for talking about me like that,' she murmured, '. . . one you will not forget in a hurry.'

Chapter Four

Some time later, Pete and Mark climbed into a taxi. Showered and shaved, they looked ready for anything.

'I hope the show is as good as everyone says.'

'Stop moaning!' Pete gave him a dig in the ribs. 'It'll be an experience if nothing else.'

Arriving at the Adelphi Theatre, they clambered out of the taxi. Mark was still grumbling as Pete paid the driver.

'If it gets boring, I'm off to the clubs!' Mark mumbled as they went inside.

'Give it a rest!' Pete strode on ahead. 'I hope you don't intend grumbling and moaning all night!'

'I'm just saying, that's all!'

'Well, you've had your say, so now shut up and enjoy.'

As it turned out, they enjoyed the show from beginning to end, and afterwards it was all they could talk about. 'That was amazing!' The two of them chatted excitedly about the great night they were having.

They hailed a passing taxi, and the grey-haired driver pulled his cab into the side of the kerb. 'Where to, mate?' he shouted through the open window.

For the first time, Mark and Pete realised they knew nothing about London clubs. They had no idea where to go, or which one might be the best. 'We're looking for a good club,' Mark told him hopefully.

'And not too expensive, because we're a bit short of cash,' Pete cut in.

The driver scratched his head. 'Get in, and we'll see what we can find, how's that?'

Half an hour later, they were driving through Soho. One by one they dismissed the clubs; one was too scruffy; one had a group of thugs hanging about outside; one was too quiet and now they were beginning to lose heart. 'Look, we're not so short of money that we can only afford the worst dive in London!' Mark groaned. 'Surely you've an idea where there's a small lively club with something going on?'

'Maybe!' The driver went to the top of the street and turned right. Half a mile further on, he stopped at a side street. 'There y' go . . . Andy's Place . . . cheap and popular, with the best music in town.'

'So why didn't you bring us here first?' Pete asked.

'Well, sometimes you might find one or two unsavoury characters lurking about and looking for trouble. Now and again a street woman might pop in looking for business if you know what I mean? . . . But as a rule, they're sent packing. So as long as you don't encourage them, you've nothing to worry about.'

Jumping out of the cab, they paid the driver and sauntered up to the front door. 'So far, this has been a great night out,' Mark laughed. 'I wouldn't mind coming back to see another show.'

Once they were inside the club however, all Mark could talk about was his chance of pulling a great-looking girl.

Having got himself and Pete a beer, Mark glanced about. 'This place is full of pretty girls.'

Clutching his pint, he turned towards the dance floor, where swarms of clubbers were writhing to the throb of the music in a weird kind of frenzy.

Eyes bright, Mark took a long, leisurely sip of his beer. 'You know what, Pete?'

'What now?'

'I reckon our luck's in tonight.' Mark peered

hopefully across the dance floor. 'It looks to me, like most of the girls are on their own, or having a girls' night out with their mates.'

Pete wiped his finger up the side of his glass to collect the leaking froth and glanced about. 'You could be right.' Licking his finger, he then put his glass to his mouth, and took a long, deep drink.

'If I had a voice like that Lee bloke from the musical, I'd have the girls falling at my feet,' Mark boasted.

Pete laughed. 'D'you reckon?'

Mark nodded. 'Too right!'

'See that girl over there?' He pointed to a blonde in skimpy white shorts and a low-cut pink top.

Pete nodded. 'You can hardly miss her.'

'Well, she's mine. So hands off!'

'She's got a bloke with her . . .' Pete pointed to the guy at the other end of the bar. 'He's only left her to get himself a pint.'

'No. You've got it wrong. He's not with *that* girl. He's with the blonde, who I think might be his sister?'

Mark shook his head. 'I don't think so.

'Just don't go pushing in where you're not wanted.'

Ignoring Pete's warning, Mark pointed to the

man again. 'Look! He's back with the dark-haired one.'

Pete nodded, 'Okay, but like I said, make sure of your ground before you make a move.'

Mark gave him a friendly shove. 'Stop worrying! I know what I'm doing. I'm not an absolute prat!'

Pete laughed. 'You could have fooled me!'

Pete went silent.

Mark thought he knew why Pete had gone quiet. 'You're still thinking about that girl on the platform, aren't you?'

'I might be.'

'You are!'

'Okay, so I am.'

Mark could not understand it. 'What's *wrong* with you? You've only seen her the once, and even *that* was from a distance! A couple of times I talked to you at the show, and you were miles away. It's like she's imprinted on your mind.'

He had never seen Pete so preoccupied. 'Either it really *is* love at first sight, or she's a witch, and she's put you under her spell.' Waving his fingers, he made a ghostly sound.

Pete warned him off. 'Don't talk rubbish!'

But Mark was worried. 'Think about it, mate. She could be married anyway. Or she might be a nasty piece of work no one would touch with a barge pole.'

Pete had already considered all these things. 'All right. You've made your point. Now change the subject, will you?'

'I'm sorry, mate,' Mark apologised. 'I was only thinking of you. I mean . . . you don't know that girl from Adam.'

'I thought I asked you to change the subject?'

'Okay, keep your hair on.' Mark knew when to stop, and he did.

'Fancy another drink?' Slapping a fiver into Mark's hand, Pete asked, 'Get me a lager, will you?'

Downing his pint, Mark brought two more. 'We'll finish these and wait a few minutes. Then I'm thinking I should make a move on the blonde girl.'

Pete went along with the idea. 'Right! You go for her, and I'll chat up the other one.'

'Like I said . . . it's our lucky night.'

'Okay, okay!' Pete gestured towards the dance-floor. 'The bloke's back!'

Mark was curious. 'Look there! He's brought the dark-haired one back with him.' Now all three were dancing together.

'Best leave them to it then, eh?' Pete said. 'We don't want to start world war three.'

While Mark was watching the three of them, a young auburn-haired girl was watching *him*. After a while she caught his eye and smiled at him.

'Hey, Pete!' Mark couldn't help grinning. 'Did you see that? I pulled without even trying!'

While Mark danced with the auburn-haired girl, Pete was content to stay on the sidelines and watch. He was fascinated by the other three. One minute the bloke was dancing with the blonde, and the next he was dancing with the dark-haired girl.

Wandering to the far end of the bar, he sat on the stool, lost in thoughts of that lonely girl seated on the platform bench. He could not understand why he was so smitten with her. She hadn't even looked at him. But *something* had drawn him to her, and now he couldn't think about anything else.

'Maybe Mark is right,' he thought aloud, 'maybe she really *is* a witch.'

'I hope you're not talking about *me*?' A soft voice invaded his thoughts.

Startled, he swung round to see a pretty face looking up at him. Tall and willowy, she was wearing white jeans and a dark, fitted top that followed her every curve. 'I'm sorry . . .' he smiled down at her, 'I was just thinking aloud.'

The girl moved closer. 'So, who's this witch you were talking about?'

Pete felt foolish. 'Oh, it's just some girl.'

'Not a witch then?' Her eyes seemed to melt right into his.

He gave a soft, nervous laugh. 'I hope not.'

'Who is she then?'

Pete shrugged. 'Like I said . . . she's just a girl.'

'Is she *your* girl?'

'No.' But oh, how he wished she was.

Encouraged, she closed in on him. 'Do you have a girlfriend?'

Pete shook his head. 'Not at the minute, no.'

'Are you looking for someone?'

He gazed down at the pretty face and wondered if she was just playing games with him. 'I might be. Why? Are you offering?'

She smiled. 'You never know.'

'Would you like a drink?'

'Thank you, no.' She leaned towards him. 'You can ask me if I need a *friend* though.'

'Well, do you . . . need a friend, I mean?'

'Why?' She had a definite look in her eye. 'Do you want to be my friend?'

Pete shrugged. 'That depends.'

'On what?'

'On whether you're using me to make a boyfriend jealous. Are you?'

She laughed out loud. 'Aren't you the cagey one?'

'You still haven't answered my question.'

She shifted nearer. 'Look . . .' Laying her hand on his arm, she told him quietly but firmly, 'I do *not* have a boyfriend. Nor am I the kind of girl who would use one man, to get at another.'

She took hold of his hand and drew him off the stool. Without a word, she led him across the room, and through the door on the far side.

Pete went with her willingly. He could feel the warmth of her hand in his; but it was the other girl who filled his thoughts.

From across the dance floor Mark was surprised to see them leave. 'Where's *he* off to?'

'Who?' The auburn-haired girl followed Mark's gaze, in time to see Pete and the girl leaving.

'That's my mate,' Mark explained. 'I just wondered where he was going with that girl'

'Her name is Maggie,' she told him with a giggle. 'She's the landlord's daughter, and that door leads to their private quarters.' Snuggling up to him, she whispered, 'I hope your friend knows what he's doing, because I hear Maggie has a *huge* appetite . . . if you know what I mean?'

Mark laughed. 'In that case, she'll probably take his mind off that other woman.'

'What other woman'

'A woman he hasn't even met yet.'

'What do you mean?'

Mark smiled at her. 'Never you mind.'

They enjoyed the music and the dancing, and when Mark commented on Pete being gone for so long, she laughed. 'I *told* you Maggie had a huge appetite.'

'What about *you?*' he asked. 'What's your appetite like?'

'Good enough, I expect.'

'So, do you fancy going through that door?'

'Nope.'

'Why not?'

'Because my boyfriend's just arrived, and I'd hate for him to beat the pulp out of you.' With that, she ran over to where the guy was already making a beeline for Mark, an ominous expression on his face and his fists clenched tight.

Mark might have squared up to him, but one look told him to back off. 'Oh, God!' Over six feet tall with bulging muscles, the 'boyfriend' was baying for blood. 'Time to go!'

He began a hasty exit towards the main door, but the guy beat him to it. 'In a hurry are we?'

45

'Leave him alone!' The auburn-haired girl got between the two of them. 'He's no threat to you,' she yelled, '. . . *he's gay*.'

'Like hell he is!' The blond guy with the two girls pushed his way through. 'I've been watching this creep! He's not gay. He's been eyeing my girls all night. I'll teach him a lesson he'll never forget!'

Before he could get to Mark, an almighty noise erupted from overhead. There was the sound of a woman's voice screaming, and what seemed like furniture being thrown about. 'That's Maggie!' The barman set off at a run towards the private quarters. 'Quick, she's at it again!'

Pandemonium followed, with everyone running up the stairs with Mark in front. 'Run for it, Pete!' he kept on shouting. 'Run for it!' Then somebody clapped him round the ear and deafened him.

Upstairs, the barman put his shoulder to the door and burst into the room. There was Maggie, with Pete at her mercy.

Handcuffed to the bed, his shirt torn to shreds and his trousers round his ankles, Pete looked terrified. 'Get her off me!' he screamed, 'she's a bloody maniac!'

There was an outburst of laughter as the barman wrenched them apart. 'I've told you before . . .' he warned Maggie, '. . . some men don't enjoy the things you do. Now unlock the handcuffs and behave yourself.' Pete lurched off the bed and the barman threw him across the room. When Pete's trousers tripped him up, the bloke with the two girls dragged him to his feet and slung him head-first onto the landing.

'Take your poncy friend and don't ever show your faces here again!' Grabbing Pete and Mark by the scruff of the neck, the bloke sent them crashing down the stairs. They landed in a heap at the bottom, and the bloke called a warning. 'If I do see you again, we'll lock you both inside and let Maggie loose on you.'

As the pair fled down the street, with Pete tripping and falling as he tried to pull up his trousers, the sound of hearty laughter echoed after them.

'Taxi!' The B&B was close enough to walk to, but they needed a quick getaway. By the time Mark hailed a taxi, Pete had managed to pull up his trousers. 'Leila's guest house, and hurry please.' Mark dragged Pete into the taxi. 'My mate here is feeling a little worse for wear.' He laughed out loud.

The driver grinned to himself. He recognised the signs – hair standing on end; the bewildered look and the trousers at half-mast.

He glanced at Pete through his driving mirror. 'Looks to me like you've had a tussle with our Maggie.'

'You could say that,' Pete zipped up his trousers, 'how did you guess?'

'Let's just say, we've all been there.'

Frantically running his hands through his hair, Pete played it cool. 'I don't want to talk about it,' he said. 'Just get me away from here.'

'That's enough!' While Mark fell about laughing, Pete was not amused. 'Just shut it! Get me back to the B&B.'

The landlady was waiting at the door. 'You look like you had a good night!' she taunted as Pete hobbled in. 'Ooh! You didn't meet Mad Maggie by any chance, did you?'

When Mark slyly nodded, she gave Pete a wicked smile. 'Oh, dear! I could have warned you about her. That one has a bad reputation, for bringing the men down to size ... so to speak.'

'I've no idea what you're talking about.' Pete gave her a shrivelling glance as he headed for the stairs. 'I know nothing about any Mad Maggie!'

'Goodnight,' she said cheerily, 'sleep well.'

Mark hung about, looking at her with sheep's

eyes, wanting to say something, but lacking the courage.

After locking the door behind them, she gave Mark a little wink and was quickly gone.

'Did you see that?' Mark said, catching Pete up on the stairs.

'See *what*?' Pete was in no mood for conversation.

'She winked at me!'

'Don't be daft!' Pete tripped up the step. 'She probably had a speck of dirt in her eye.'

'No! You're wrong. She really fancies me.'

Pete continued to crawl up the stairs. 'Rather you than me! I'm finished with women from now on.'

'What about that girl on the platform then?'

Pete shrugged. In fact, thinking about the girl on the platform was the only way he had kept sane while Maggie was taking him apart.

'Will you be all right?' Mark wondered, as he escorted Pete to his room. 'Do you need me to stay in with you tonight?'

Pete leapt to his feet. 'Do I hell! The last thing I need is to wake up with a bloke!'

'Don't *you* start!' Mark's feelings were hurt. 'You ungrateful sod! I'm only looking out for you.'

'Sorry. I really am grateful, but I'm okay. Once I'm in that bed, I'll be out like a light.'

'Right, well, if you feel ill in the night, come and get me.'

'There'll be no need for that.' Wincing, Pete gingerly touched his ribcage. 'Though to tell you the truth, I reckon she might have broken a few bones.'

'Shouldn't we go to hospital . . . get you checked out?'

'What, and have them question me? I don't think so!'

'Goodnight then . . . or should I say Good morning.' He glanced at his watch. '*It's half past midnight.*'

'This business about Mad Maggie, and all that . . .'

Mark grinned. 'What about it?'

'I want you to promise that you'll never talk about it to anyone back home.'

'If that's what you want.' Mark chuckled.

'I want you to promise!'

'I've already *said*, haven't I?'

'Not properly. I want you to promise!'

Mark groaned. 'Give it a rest!'

Terrified, Pete grabbed him by the lapels. 'You're not to say anything. Promise me, dammit!'

'Okay, okay! If that's what you want.'

'It is.'

'Then I promise.' Mark shook himself free and started chuckling again. 'It *was* funny though. You should have seen your face – hand-cuffed to the bed like that . . .' When he saw the menacing look on Pete's face he stood back. 'All right, all right! I won't tell a soul!'

Pete nodded. 'Thanks, mate.'

'What for?'

'For getting me back, and giving me your word, and all that.'

Mark strolled away. 'See you in the morning then?'

Pete grinned. 'The way I'm hurting, I might never wake up.'

'You'd better wake up,' Mark said, '. . . you've got the train-tickets home, *and* our last tenner.'

Chapter Five

It was in the early hours when Mark sensed he was not alone. Leila slid into his bed and suddenly they were entwined in each other's arms. They kissed tenderly but then in a rush of passion they were making love.

In the morning she was gone, and Mark couldn't decide whether it had really happened, or if it was all a dream.

He washed and dressed and called in on Pete who was busy collecting his things together. 'You'll never guess what happened to me,' Mark told him.

Aching from top to bottom, Pete reluctantly humoured him. 'I can see you're itching to tell me . . . so go on then, what happened?'

'I had a visitor.' Mark's face melted with the memory of it. 'Oh, mate! It was something else, I'm telling you.' Coming closer, he lowered his voice. 'I spent the night with the Italian goddess. She came into my room last night, into my *bed!*'

Dropping his jacket on the bed, Pete was

open-mouthed. 'What! You mean . . . you . . .'
He gave a little grin, '. . . you and her? You
actually *did it* . . . I mean, you and her . . . in
the bed, *together*?'

'That's right. Me and her . . . in the bed.' He
rolled his eyes and grinned. 'It was really something!'

Pete laughed out loud. 'You're kidding me?'

'Nope!' Mark shook his head. 'She was
amazing! I've never known anything like it.'

Pete didn't know whether to believe him or
not, especially when they went downstairs
for breakfast and Leila completely ignored
Mark.

'I'm glad you enjoyed your stay,' she told
Pete, as the two boys were about to leave.

'Will I see you again?' Mark whispered.

'I'm afraid not,' Leila replied coldly, 'I'm
selling up and moving to Italy.'

'But . . . we . . . I mean . . .' He lowered his
voice. 'Are you saying it didn't mean anything
to you?'

She replied with a stony stare. 'Goodbye.
Have a safe journey.' She opened the door and
stepped back, allowing them to pass. When
they were gone she quietly closed the door, and
returned to her ledger.

* * *

'I don't understand it.' Mark was confused. 'How could she do that? How could she come into my bed, make love to me then treat me like a total stranger?'

Feeling miserable, he glanced at Pete. 'Do you think it *was* a dream after all?'

Pete thought so. 'It *must* have been a dream. Either that, or she was sleepwalking. I've heard of how people do things in their sleep, and afterwards they can't remember a thing about it.'

'Well, *I'll* never forget.'

'Like I said . . . that's because you remember it, and she doesn't.'

'So, she really *was* there then?'

'If you say so, I suppose she was.' Though Pete found it hard to believe.

'She really was sleepwalking, is that what you're saying?'

'I don't know Mark, it seems so'.

They travelled by taxi to Euston station, which was already heaving with people.

Pete remarked that everyone seemed in an unusually good mood. Some of them even turned to smile as Mark and Pete went by.

Mark wasn't aware of any of it. He was too busy recalling the heavenly night he'd enjoyed.

Pete let his thoughts drift back to the girl on the platform.

It was when they were boarding the train that Pete realised why people had been so amused and interested in them.

Mark was the first to climb onto the train, and Pete was horrified to see a note written on the back of Mark's jacket. In Tippex Leila had had her revenge:

> YOU'RE A LOUSY LOVER,
> YOU SNORE LIKE A PIG
> I HOPE I NEVER SEE YOU AGAIN

Falling into his seat, Pete doubled up laughing, but he didn't know what to do. Should he tell Mark, or was it best to leave it and let him find out for himself? He decided not to say anything.

Mark was confused. 'What the hell's wrong with you?'

'Nothing.'

'Have I got egg on my face or what?'

'No, not that I can see. Why?'

'Because you keep looking at me and sniggering!'

'You're imagining things. I was just thinking about that Maggie woman.' Pete had been genuinely frightened. 'Do you realize, she could have ruined me for any other woman.'

'It serves you right for sneaking off with her in the first place.'

The journey home was a nightmare, with Mark rattling on about how beautiful Leila was, and how cold she'd been to him that morning. 'I reckon she's playing tricks with me. You know what! I've a good mind to go back and give her a piece of my mind!'

While Mark chatted on, Pete fought with his conscience. It was hard not to tell Mark about the writing on his jacket. It was even harder for him not to laugh. At the same time, Pete also couldn't stop dreaming about the girl on the platform and how deeply she has crept into his thoughts.

After they got off the train, Pete offered his jacket to Mark. 'Why would I want *your* jacket when I've got my own?' Mark was curious at Pete's strange mood.

'My jacket's longer. I thought you might be cold, that's all.'

'I'm absolutely fine. You're in a weird mood. I reckon Mad Maggie must have put something in your drink.'

Out on the platform, surrounded by people, the sniggering began again. 'Don't you worry about it, son. I dare say you'll learn as you get older,' a fat woman told Mark as she waddled by.

Her male partner had his say too. 'A man needs to stay one step ahead,' he advised, 'we've got to keep women in their place!'

A group of girls giggled as they ran past. 'We've met a few like you . . . *loser!*'

'Too right!' Her mate made a V sign at him. 'Us girls have to stick together.'

'What's wrong with them?' Mark was puzzled.

'Search me.'

'I'm sure that girl meant the V sign for me!'

'Don't talk daft!' Pete wanted to get him home as quickly as possible. 'Why would she do that? The V sign had nothing to do with you and me. I bet she's had a bad experience and doesn't like men . . . *any* men, full stop!'

Mark was not convinced. 'To tell you the truth, I'm going off women fast,' he grumbled. 'They're a different breed.'

When they arrived at Mark's home, Pete shoved him in through the door and made a hasty retreat. 'Aren't you coming in?' Mark couldn't understand Pete's behaviour. In fact he was beginning to think that people as a whole were strange.

'No thanks, mate.' Pete was off at a run. 'Got to go! See you later.'

A few minutes later, just as Pete was turning the corner at the bottom of the street, he heard Mark shouting from the doorstep, 'Hey! I thought you were a mate ... more fool me! Why didn't you tell me, instead of letting me walk about looking like a first class idiot!'

From behind Mark came the sound of hysterical laughter as his family saw Leila's message.

Mark's angry voice echoed down the street. 'I won't forgive you for this!'

Pete however, had no doubt that sooner or later he would be forgiven.

Chapter Six

Late on Sunday night, Pete was lolling in front of the television, his mind wandering back over recent events. Large in his thoughts was the memory of the girl on the platform.

Try as he might, he could not shake her image out of his mind. 'I've got to pluck up courage and speak with her . . . find out who she is, and whether we could go out sometime.' The idea of taking her out on a date warmed him right through.

The shrill tone of the telephone echoed through the room, snapping Pete out of his quiet thoughts. It was Mark. 'I'm sorry, mate,' he apologised. 'I shouldn't have come down hard on you like that . . . it wasn't *your* fault, it was mine. Anyway, I don't suppose there was much you could have done about that damned thing she wrote on my coat,' he confessed. 'It was my own stupid fault for getting involved with a woman out of my league.'

Pete had his own regrets. 'Put it down to experience,' he suggested. 'Leila was still out of order though, doing what she did. I didn't have the heart to tell you, and besides, what could either of us have done, even if I *had* told you?'

'I dunno. Taken off my jacket for a start.' Mark felt such a fool. 'I suppose I'm a bit upset because I really liked her, and I thought she liked me.'

'Don't delude yourself,' Pete warned. 'She's like all the others, out for what she can get and then to hell with you.'

'You know what?' Mark was finding it hard to come to terms with what she had done to him.

'What?'

'I've a good mind to write to her.'

'I wouldn't bother if I were you. Anyway, after she made a fool of you like that, why would you want to write to her?'

'To ask her why she did it?' A quiet smile flitted across Mark's face. 'It would be interesting to see if she writes back.'

'Rather you than me!' Pete needed to put the whole episode behind him. 'How about if we meet up for a drink after work tomorrow?'

'Okay.' Mark was all for that. 'Sounds good to me.'

As arranged, they met up the following night, laughed at their ordeals, and as they walked home from the pub, they made a pact not to tell anyone about their sad escapade in London.

'I've had the worst day at work ever,' Mark said. 'We had a whole fleet of lorries in for servicing, and six new arrivals to get ready for the road. On top of that, we've got two men down with the flu.' He sighed. 'Even with all that going on, all I could think of was Leila. Honest to God, Pete, I've never met anyone like her.'

'Get over it, Mark!' Pete warned him. 'It was never going anywhere, and you know it.'

'I expect you're right.' Mark's voice trailed off as he started to feel a bit embarrassed.

Realising that Pete was watching him, he loudly declared, 'But if she thinks she's got the better of me, she can think again. I'll put her right out of my mind, that's what I'll do! I've got enough to think about at work, without fretting over some woman who gets a kick out of sleeping with men then dropping them like they never happened!'

Even so, he had not given up on the idea of writing to her. In fact, he meant to do just that the minute he got home.

He turned to Pete. '*You're* not saying much.'

'That's because you've said it all.'

'Changing the subject are you? Okay, so how did your day go at work?'

Pete shrugged. 'Much the same as yours.' 'We've had a rush on all day. That new development at the top of Bridge Street has just been released, and there was a list of viewings as long as your arm. Some of the viewers were complete timewasters. I've had little more than an hour in the office, so what with the paperwork piling up, and countless phone messages, I had to work right through my break. I don't mind telling you, mate, I'm shattered!'

Mark had an idea. 'Why don't we both take the day off tomorrow? You ring up and tell my boss I'm down with the flu, then I'll do the same for you.'

'I can't.' Pete would have liked to though. 'The manager's away on a course all day. We're far too busy for me to skive off. Besides, I'm looking for promotion this year. We're opening a country home department, and there's three of us after the job.'

'No worries. You're bound to get it. You said yourself, you sell more properties than anyone in that company.'

'You're right, I do, you don't always get your just rewards. This new department is worth a fortune to the man who can deliver the goods.

What I make now is nothing to the commission I could make there.'

'How's that?' Mark could turn a car engine inside out, and sell a new car to somebody who only came in to have a look, but he didn't know the first thing about selling houses. 'How can you make more money selling one house against another?'

'Think about it,' Pete said, 'one country property might be worth what . . . half a million quid? I'd have to sell three or four small properties in town to get the same commission. Do you see what I'm saying?'

'Wow!' Mark was impressed. 'I see what you mean. I still think you're the best man for the job, so just go for it!'

They parted at the bottom of Craig Street. 'See you then,' Mark told him.

Pete gave him a friendly wave as he went away, wishing he could win the lottery.

The following morning Pete looked hard at himself in the bathroom mirror. 'With a bit of luck, today might be the day when you get to chat with the girl on the platform.'

A minute later he rushed downstairs, passing his mother, who was in the kitchen putting on her lipstick. 'See you tonight,' he called.

'Make sure you're home in time for dinner,' she told him. 'No going round to see Mark before you get home.'

He went out of the house and hurried down to the station, where he stood patiently on the platform, waiting for his train. It arrived ten minutes late, as usual.

The girl didn't show that day, or the next, and Pete began to worry. 'Where *is* she?' he wondered. 'What's happened to her?'

On Friday, she was there, and it was like the sun had come out after days of gloom.

He saw her twice again that following week; both times she was on the opposite platform. She was on her own, and Pete toyed with the idea of missing his train to cross over and speak with her, but at the last minute he lost his nerve. 'Next time,' he promised himself, 'I'll pluck up the courage.'

The next time though, she appeared to be waiting for someone to get off the train. The man she met looked to be about thirty. His face lit up with joy when he caught sight of her and when they hugged, it was like he would never let her go.

All that day, Pete found it hard to concentrate on his work. He burned with jealousy, and love, and hated the man who had dared to hold her so tightly. His mind was forever wandering. 'Wake up, you mug!' he told himself. 'You mean *nothing* to her.' But it made no difference. He needed to know who she was, and whether he stood any kind of a chance with her.

The following week was a nightmare. He looked for her on the way to work, and he looked for her on the way back, and in between she filled his thoughts, until he was sure he might go mad.

He couldn't sleep or eat, and when his father asked if he was sickening for something, Pete told him he was fine. But he *was* sickening for something. He was sickening for the girl.

He told himself she might be the most awful person on earth if he ever got to talk with her. She could be a man hater, but then why would she throw herself into that other man's arms if that was the case? And even if she was *all* of these things, he still wanted to know her, to hear her voice and look into her eyes. But how? When?

Somewhere deep inside him, he knew she was the girl for him. He had to believe that she was not married. But, who was the guy that she met at the station?

Chapter Seven

On Saturday, night, Pete and Mark met for a drink at the local. Mark was horrified at Pete's appearance. 'You look bloody awful! That's twice you've not heard when I've been talking to you, and you look as though you could do with a good night's sleep. Are you ill, or what?'

Pete gave him a sheepish look. 'Don't laugh, but . . . I think I'm in love.'

'What!' Mark laughed out loud. 'Don't give me that! You haven't met anybody to be in love with. So, who is she, this phantom lover?'

It was a moment before Pete answered. 'It's the girl on the platform,' he said quietly. 'I can't get her out of my mind. I keep seeing her; she's there one minute and then she's gone, and the other day, she met a guy off the train. They hugged for ages. He seemed to be really important to her. It drove me crazy! I couldn't work and since then, all I can think of is *her*.'

Desperation was written all over his face.

'I know it sounds crazy, but I just can't get her out of my mind, and I don't know what to do about it.'

Mark was a straightforward guy and he could not understand how anybody could fall so head over heels in love with a complete stranger; though he had to admit that Leila had been on his mind more than he would have liked. 'Pete! Get a grip! You've never even met this girl,' he said. 'How can you be *in love* with her?'

'Don't know, but I am.'

Mark disagreed. 'You can't be! Okay, you might be infatuated. Don't we always want something we can't have ... look at me, with Leila. I really wanted it to go somewhere, but she was only using me. You won't see me hankering and mooning after her, and that's because I've moved on.' He gave a smug little smile. 'Matter of fact, I've got my eye on a girl we saw in the pub the other night.'

'That's because you go from one woman to another, and most of the time it's you using *them*.'

'You're the same.'

'Not any more. Not after seeing her.'

'All right then ...' Mark gave a long, heavy

sigh. 'I can see you've got it bad, so the way I see it now, you've got two choices.'

Pete sat up to listen. 'Go on!'

'You've got to get her out of your mind!'

'I can't!'

'Then you'll drive yourself crazy. Look at me, Pete! Do you see *me* fretting over Leila? No, you don't, and that's because I'm determined not to let her destroy my peace of mind and, like it or not, you have to do the same.'

'That's not an option. So, what's the second choice?'

Mark shrugged. '*Find her.*'

'How can I do that?'

'I've no idea. That's for you to work out, and if you ask me, the sooner the better.'

All weekend, Pete was on edge.

On Monday morning, as he was about to leave for work, his father followed him to the front door. 'What's wrong, son?' His dad had noticed how agitated Pete had been since coming home from London.

Pete thought he'd managed to hide his frustration from his parents. 'Nothing. Why are you asking?' he replied with an air of innocence.

'I'm asking, because your mother says you've

nearly worn the bedroom carpet bare with pacing up and down. Also, you've gone off your food. Now, as I see it, there are two possible reasons for that.'

'Oh, so you're the expert are you?'

The older man shook his head. 'No, son. I'm your father, and though it might seem impossible to you, I was a young man once, much like yourself. I can see all the signs.'

'Right, so if you know so much, you can tell *me* what the problem is?'

'You've missed the promotion at work. I know you wanted it bad, son, and I'm sorry if you missed out, but you'll get there, maybe not this time, but soon.'

'You're wrong. The promotion hasn't been decided yet.'

His dad smiled knowingly. 'Then you must be in love.'

For a moment Pete was quiet, and oddly embarrassed. He loved his dad, but they had never discussed anything personal, and certainly not either of their love-lives.

'Well, am I right, or am I right?'

Pete nodded. 'I've seen this girl. She sometimes sits on the platform waiting for the train. Oh, Dad! She's so lovely, and so sad, and I'd give anything to find out who she is.'

69

His dad nodded knowingly. He had been there himself many years ago. 'Why don't you then?' he asked. 'Go and talk with her . . . tell her how you've admired her from afar.'

'I can't!'

'Why not?'

'Because she might think I'm a weirdo and make a run for it. Then I'll *never* get to know her!'

'You know what they say, don't you, son?'

'What's that, Dad?'

'"Faint heart never won fair lady," and it's true.' He smiled at Pete. 'Talk to her. She'll either like you, or she won't. At least you'll know and then you might stop driving yourself crazy, and we'll *all* get some peace.'

All the way to the station and even when he was on the train, Pete thought about his dad's words. 'He's right! The next time I see her, I'll go across and talk to her. I will!' He felt good. 'I don't even care if it makes me late for work. What's a promotion compared to knowing her?'

He stared out the window, his eyes glued to the opposite platform, watching for her, waiting for his opportunity. If she arrived, he was going to leap off the train and go over to her. There was still time, he thought.

Minutes passed, and there was no sign of her, and he knew she would not show that morning. 'Tomorrow she'll be there, I know she will!' Bitterly disappointed, he settled in his seat.

But when the train engine began revving up ready to leave, he glanced out the window and his heart almost stopped. It was her! She and another girl were running along the platform . . . *his platform!*

She looked so lovely, dressed in a blue jacket and full, dark skirt; she was carrying a black handbag with a large pink and blue flower embroidered on the side. Her high-heeled black shoes gave her ankles a slender look, and when she walked, the hem of her skirt swung to reveal a pair of shapely legs. And just now, when the sunlight fell on her hair, it shone like newly fallen chestnuts.

The two girls clambered onto the train just before the doors shut. When they sat down two rows in front of him, Pete was so nervous he didn't know what to do. He couldn't take his eyes off her. From where he sat he could only see the back of her head, and when she turned to speak with her friend, he could just see the smallest part of her profile.

He could hear her voice, soft and warm,

though when she laughed at her friend's sorry little jokes, he could detect the slightest sense of sadness, which touched him deeply.

He thought of what his dad had said . . . 'Talk to her, son'. That had been his advice, and now Pete simply had to act on it.

When the train came to a halt at the next stop, other passengers got up to leave. He got up with them, but moved only as far as the seat behind the girls. He hoped they would not notice, and they didn't.

It lifted his spirits to see her smiling. 'You're even more lovely than I remember,' he murmured.

In fact, Pete thought she was the loveliest thing he had ever seen, and he knew he would not rest until he knew who she was.

Unashamed, Pete tried to memorise every word of their conversation.

'I miss him so much.' That was his lovely girl.

'I know,' her friend replied softly, 'when you love like that, you can't bear to be without them.'

'He was so wonderful . . . waiting to cuddle and kiss me when I got back, and . . .' her voice broke, 'I'm sorry, Liz, but I really need him with me right now.'

Pete was getting hot under the collar. He

recalled the guy who had taken her so lovingly in his arms when he got off the train, and how delighted she was to see him. Now, it seemed to Pete that the girl had been dumped. If he could get his hands on that devil, he'd teach him a lesson.

What were they saying now?

'You've got to get over him,' the friend was saying, 'you're making yourself ill.'

'I know that, but it's so awful without him. When I get home and open the front door, he's not there, his little tail wagging and those big adoring eyes looking up at me. He gave me such affection and love, and never asked for anything in return.'

Her voice broke; she wiped her eyes and apologised again. 'You're right,' she told her friend, 'I know it's only a dog, but I had him from a puppy when I was ten years old. Twelve years I had him, and he was my best friend. Whenever anything went wrong in my life, he was always there to help me pick up the pieces.'

'Can I ask you something, Mary?' her friend said.

Mary nodded. 'Course you can.'

'Would it help to get a puppy ... another border terrier like Jasper?'

Mary shook her head. 'I don't think so,' she answered quietly. 'I miss him too much to even think of replacing him.'

For a while they were quiet with their thoughts. Then they were talking about shopping and work. 'That was good of Sally Parker to let you have the day off,' her friend told Mary, 'she's such a nice person.'

'Yes, she is,' Mary agreed. 'She said I should take a day off, especially after that rush we had on yesterday. We had six wedding bouquets to prepare, and about eighteen different bridesmaid bouquets.'

She gave a long, weary sigh. 'What with that building work going on right outside the Harpur Centre, it's taking us all our time to keep the dust out of the shop. I can't help feeling guilty, leaving her on her own today.'

'But today's not so hard is it? I mean, you did all the hard work yesterday, and Monday is always quiet in Bedford.'

'Yes, but don't forget she let me have the day off the other week, when my brother came down to stay with me.'

Pete was so excited he wanted to shout for joy. Her name was *Mary!* Lovely, wonderful *Mary!* The name suited her like no other could.

What's more, the guy from the train was her *brother*, and not her boyfriend! His heart was pounding, and he felt as though he'd won the lottery after all!

When the train stopped at Bletchley, the girls remained on board while Pete got off, his mind buzzing with an idea.

Chapter Eight

Pete arrived at the office all nervous and excited. 'Is my car back from its service?' he asked the secretary.

'Not till Friday,' she told him. 'That's why you've been given local appointments.'

'Will you do me a swap?' he asked his colleague; a tall thin man called Tim, 'I really need to be in Leighton Buzzard.'

Tim had a smile that would frighten the devil. 'Suppose I could.'

'It's that first appointment . . . the one at the old vicarage just down the road?'

'What's it worth?'

'Lunch and a bottle of wine to take home.'

Tim's face lit up. 'Go on then.'

'Thanks!' Pete was over the moon. 'I owe you one.'

'I won't let you forget it neither,' Tim drawled. 'Do you need your car?'

'How long do you want it for?'

'An hour at most. It's *really* important.'

'Okay. No more than an hour, or I can't do

my other appointments.' Digging into his pocket he threw Pete the keys. 'Anyway, what's so special about Leighton Buzzard?'

Pete grabbed his appointment book and hurried out the door. 'Tell you later!' he said as he ran.

It took him fifteen minutes to get to Leighton Buzzard, where he parked the car and ran up the slope. There was a pet shop halfway down the high street. 'Quick!' Running inside he accosted the nearest salesperson. 'I'd like to see some puppies.'

Startled, the girl said, 'We're not allowed to keep animals on the premises, but we might be able to get you a puppy. What kind are you looking for?'

Pete had to think. 'What did she say?' he mumbled. 'Some sort of terrier, I think.'

'Was it a Jack Russell?'

'No.'

'A Scottie?'

'No.'

'Well, I'm sorry, I can't help you if you don't know what kind of breed you want.'

Pete thought and thought, turning the conversation over in his mind. 'She asked why didn't Mary get another puppy . . . a terrier of some sort, I remember *that*.' He groaned, 'terrier . . . terrier . . .' Suddenly it clicked and he yelled out loud, 'Border terrier! That was it . . . a *border* terrier.' He could hardly contain his excitement.

The assistant went onto the computer and located a breeder almost straightaway. 'They have two left,' she told Pete. 'A bitch and a dog. Can you remember which one she wanted?'

Pete could easily remember that. 'A dog!' He knew that because when she referred to 'him', he thought she was talking about the guy she met off the train. 'I'll take the dog. When will it be here? When will I be able to collect it?'

'I could get it here for you on Friday, if you want to pay for the pick-up. Otherwise it will be next week when they deliver.'

Pete paid the five pounds and went away happy.

Back in Bletchley he gave Tim his car keys, embarked on his local appointments and took Tim down the road for lunch. He watched him down three burgers and two apple pies, in the time it took Pete to eat one chicken burger. On the way out, he bought a bottle of red wine and Tim was delighted.

When Friday came, he collected his company

car and headed straight for his first appointment, which he got through in record time.

After that he went to the pet shop and there he collected the sweetest little puppy, dark brown with floppy ears and big wet eyes. 'He's just what I wanted!' Never having had a pet, he was entranced when it licked his face.

'He's not been named,' said the girl, 'so he answers to anything at the minute. Also, he's already toilet trained so he's not likely to pee on your lap.'

Pete thanked her. Then he bought every accessory imaginable to keep the puppy content; a dog basket, a leash and collar, a coat in case it got cold, and everything else the woman recommended.

He placed the dog and dog basket in the back seat of his car and headed for Bedford. 'We're going to see the prettiest girl you've ever clapped eyes on,' he told the puppy, who was curled up fast asleep.

The journey to Bedford took him through Woburn Sands and Aspley Guise, then over the M1 junction and on towards Bedford. It was a straight road all the way into Kempston, then a quick dash through the town and into Bedford. 'What was it she said . . . ?' He cast his mind back, '... building work going on at the Harpur Centre ... dust going into the shop, that's what she said.'

Pete got as close as possible to the Harpur Centre.

'Come on you!' Tenderly lifting the lazy puppy into his arms, he wrapped it close to him. He then locked the car and walked along the embankment and into the Centre.

Once inside the Centre he located Sally Parker's flower shop. It was a pretty place, in a busy thoroughfare. 'Here we are,' he declared, whispering to the puppy, 'I'm hoping we can find you a pretty new owner and a warm loving home.'

As he walked in through the door, his heart sank. Mary was nowhere in sight. 'Good morning, can I help you?' The cheery voice belonged to a kindly looking woman who was busy arranging flowers in a bucket.

Pausing for a quick breath, Pete explained, 'I've just found a puppy abandoned, and I was wondering if you or your colleague could tell me if there's a rescue centre near here.' He would have gone on, but at the sound of his voice Mary appeared. *His* Mary.

'Where is it now?' she said.

'Where is *what*?' Pete was momentarily confused.

'The puppy!' Mary came round from behind the counter. 'Where's the *puppy*?'

Standing there, with Mary looking up at him with soft brown eyes and an expression of dismay on her face, Pete could hardly restrain himself from kissing her.

'Well?'

'Oh, yes, the puppy. He was shivering, so I thought it best to keep him warm.' He opened his jacket and drew out the smallest bundle of fur and paws. 'He's such a tiny little thing, I really don't know how any one could be so cruel!'

Mary gasped, 'Oh look! He's just like Jasper!' Her eyes filled with tears as she drew the puppy into her arms. 'He's so lovely . . . same colour, and those big sad eyes . . . just like my Jasper!' Looking up at Pete, she laughed and she cried, and before he realised what he was doing, he had her in his arms and she was crying all over his jacket. But he didn't care. *He had her in his arms*. The girl on the platform in his arms! He could hardly believe it.

Together they went into the back room, and he held the puppy while she got it a saucer of water. Pete watched as she helped the puppy to drink, and his heart was full.

Mary was everything he had dreamed she

might be. She was kind and thoughtful, and she had the warmest, prettiest eyes he had ever seen.

He was glad he'd plucked up the courage to come here, because now he knew beyond a shadow of doubt that he loved her.

But how did *Mary* feel? Did she feel anything for him, or was she just grateful that he had taken care of the puppy?

'Please . . .' Mary's voice was gentle, 'can I have him?'

Pete found himself speechless again.

'I'll look after him . . . I had a little dog just like him and now that I haven't got him anymore, I'm so lonely. Please . . . I promise you, he'll have a good home, and more love than he can handle.'

She was desperate. 'Look, if you're worried, I'll give you my address and you can see for yourself. You can come back any time and make sure I'm looking after him. Oh, please! Don't take him to the rescue centre. Let me have him.'

How could he refuse?

Pete went back to Mary's little cottage with her that evening. She made him coffee and they sat down to watch the puppy play with Jasper's old toys. Mary told Pete, 'You don't know how happy you've made me.' Then she was crying again, and he was holding her, and when she looked up at him his heart leaped. The urge to kiss her was so strong.

'Don't rush it, you idiot!' he told himself. 'Or you'll frighten her away. Take it steady.' He told himself as he drove home.

He smiled inwardly. He did love her so and he wanted to go back and tell her how he felt, how he had felt from the minute he first saw her. But he knew he wouldn't. He knew he would have to be patient. It was far too important to risk losing her now.

Over the next few weeks, Pete called Mary and Mary called him, and one evening he took her out on a real date. Their first kiss was heaven, and Pete had never been happier.

Six weeks from the day he gave her the puppy, Pete asked Mary to marry him and she said yes. His life was complete.

'I love you *so* much,' she told him one evening. 'Wasn't it strange how the puppy brought us together?'

Pete said it was, though he blushed at the

way he had deceived her, and he vowed to tell her the truth before they were married. For now though, he could hardly believe that he was planning to be married to the girl on the platform.

His mother said he was lucky to have such a lovely girl, and his dad said how it was all meant to be.

Mark was chosen as best man, and he had a surprise for Pete. His date for the wedding was Leila. 'I never thought Leila would write back to me but she did,' he said proudly, 'and now I've forgiven her for writing that note on my jacket.'

Pete was happy for him. 'I can't imagine what she ever saw in you,' he laughed. 'She must be desperate! Do you realise it'll be like World War Three if you take her on permanently?'

Mark gave a knowing smile that made Pete curious. 'Don't you worry about me,' Mark grinned, 'she's met her match. You see before you a man who is quite capable of handling his woman.'

'I hope you're not talking about *me*?' A dark, sultry voice echoed across the room.

Mark jumped. 'Of course not my lovely Leila!'

He gave her a cheeky smile and held out his hand. 'Fancy a dance, d'you?'

Everyone laughed, particularly Pete and Mary, who were arm in arm, hopelessly in love.

The girl on the platform, and him!

Whoever would have thought it?

Quick Reads

Books in the Quick Reads series

www.quickreads.org.uk

Quick Reads

Pick up a book today

Quick Reads are bite-sized books by bestselling writers and well-known personalities for people who want a short, fast-paced read. They are designed to be read and enjoyed by avid readers and by people who never had or who have lost the reading habit.

Quick Reads are published alongside and in partnership with BBC RaW.

We would like to thank all our partners in the Quick Reads project for their help and support:

The Department for Innovation, Universities and Skills
NIACE
unionlearn
National Book Tokens
The Vital Link
The Reading Agency
National Literacy Trust
Welsh Books Council
Basic Skills Cymru, Welsh Assembly Government
Wales Accent Press
Lifelong Learning Scotland
DELNI
NALA

Quick Reads would also like to thank the Department for Innovation, Universities and Skills; Arts Council England and World Book Day for their sponsorship and NIACE for their outreach work.

Quick Reads is a World Book Day initiative.
www.quickreads.org.uk   www.worldbookday.com

Quick Reads

East End Tales
Gilda O'Neill

Penguin

Gilda O'Neill was born in London's East End. Her nan had a pie and mash shop and her grandfather was a tug-boat skipper. You might think Gilda's childhood was filled with knees-ups in pubs and famous criminals – but that is just half the story. In *East End Tales*, Gilda tells what the true East End was like – not the place of myth and legend. Tales of hardship and upheaval rub shoulders with stories of kindness, pride, courage and humour.

Other resources

Free courses are available for anyone who wants to develop their skills. You can attend the courses in your local area. If you'd like to find out more, phone 0800 66 0800.

 Don't get by get on 0800 66 0800

A list of books for new readers can be found on www.firstchoicebooks.org.uk or at your local library.

The
Vital
Link

Publishers Barrington Stoke (www.barringtonstoke.co.uk), New Island (www.newisland.ie) and Sandstone Press (www.sandstonepress.com) also provide books for new readers.

Barrington Stoke   OPEN DOOR   SANDSTONEPRESS
CONTEMPORARY QUALITY READING

The BBC runs a reading and writing campaign. See www.bbc.co.uk/raw.

2008 is a National Year of Reading. To find out more, search online, see www.dius.gov.uk or visit your local library.

www.quickreads.org.uk   www.worldbookday.com